BLANK

D0334019

Titles in Teen Reads:

Badger Publishing Limited, Oldmedow Road, Hardwick Industrial Estate, King's Lynn PE30 4JJ
Telephone: 01438 791037

www.badgerlearning.co.uk

BLANK

ANN EVANS

Badger LEARNING

Coventry City Council	
CEN*	
3 8002 02334 241 5	
Askews & Holts	Apr-2017
TEENAGE 11-14	£5.99

Blank ISBN 978-1-78464-621-9

Text © Ann Evans 2016
Complete work © Badger Publishing Limited 2016

All rights reserved. No part of this publication may be
reproduced, stored in any form or by any means mechanical,
electronic, recording or otherwise without the prior permission
of the publisher.

The right of Ann Evans to be identified as author of this Work has
been asserted by her in accordance with the Copyright, Designs and
Patents Act 1988.

Publisher: Susan Ross
Senior Editor: Danny Pearson
Editorial Coordinator: Claire Morgan
Copyeditor: Cambridge Publishing Management
Designer: Bigtop Design Ltd
Cover: © Blend Images / Alamy Stock Photo

2 4 6 8 10 9 7 5 3 1

CHAPTER 1

RUNNING FOR HIS LIFE

Run!

It was the only thought in Eric Penny's head. *Run!* Run like his life depended on it. Ha! His life *did* depend on it.

Blanking out the last few sickening moments, Eric ran. Long legs sprinting down lamp-lit streets, jacket flying open, heart pounding, hands sticky with blood.

He tore on, zig-zagging traffic as horns blared. Passers-by jumped out of his way, shouting angrily.

"Sorry!"

Sweat trickled into his wild eyes, bile rose in his throat. He didn't look back, didn't dare stop. Far off, a police siren wailed. Its high-pitched whine grew louder till it was screaming. In his head, *he* was screaming.

Headlights blazed, blue lights spun, blinding him.

It was all too close, too close…

His feet skidded, but it was too late…

Thud!

Now *he* was spinning — up and over the roof of the police car. Life went into slow motion. The number 101 was on its roof. 101 — the same as his house number; 101 — the number of times he'd been belted by his stepdad. And then the road rushed up to meet him.

And total blackness swamped him.

***

"He's waking up!"

A female voice drifted into Eric's foggy mind. He tried to open his eyes. Each eyelid weighed a ton. Slowly, blurred figures swayed before him. He squinted, blinked, tried to focus.

He hurt. Every bit of him hurt, like he'd been run over by a steamroller.

"Eric? Eric, how are you feeling?" A male voice now.

Eric peered up at the misty figure. Dark-skinned, white coat, something hanging round his neck. Eric squinted. It looked like a stethoscope.

The man shone a light into Eric's eyes. "Good, good. You're looking much better now, Eric."

Why were they calling him Eric? He didn't know any Erics. "Where am I?"

It hurt to talk. His throat was dry. He'd kill for a drink of water.

"You're in hospital, Eric. You've had
an accident."

They'd mixed him up with someone else. He
tried to sit up. His head felt like lead. There was a
tube in his wrist attached to a bag of clear liquid
being drip-fed into him.

"What's going on?"

The woman spoke — a nurse. She had nice eyes
— friendly eyes. "You ran into the road. A car
hit you."

He tried to make a joke. "Ah! That explains the
pain! Have I broken any bones?"

"Amazingly, no," said the doctor. "But you've had
a head injury. You've been unconscious, Eric."

Eric again. What was with the Eric thing?

The doctor went on. "In fact, you've been out of
it for quite a while."

"Must have needed a snooze," he joked, smiling at the nurse.

She held his hand. For a moment he thought his charm had worked. Then he saw the look on her face and sensed bad news.

"You've been in a coma," said the doctor. "These last 16 days."

His mouth dropped open. "What? You're winding me up!"

He couldn't have slept for two weeks. What about eating, drinking, going to the loo? Then, feeling under the bed sheets, he felt the tubes.
He blushed.

"That's more like it," said the nurse giving him a cheeky wink. "You've got a bit of colour in your cheeks now."

"Do you remember the car hitting you, Eric?" asked the doctor. "The police car?"

This was crazy. "No I don't remember a police car. And I'm not Eric. I haven't a clue who Eric is." His voice rose. "Why do you keep calling me Eric?"

"It's your name," said the doctor, frowning. "Are you saying you don't remember who you are?"

He tried to think straight. This was stupid. "Hang on. It'll come to me."

They waited. Nothing came.

Finally, the nurse said, "Your parents have been in. You *are* Eric Penny, aged 15, a pupil at St John's High." She glanced at the doctor. "I'll ring them again. Let them know he's out of the coma."

That bugged him. If *he* had a kid unconscious and in a coma, he'd be by their side every minute, day or night. So where were they — his parents?

His head was starting to throb. He tried to picture his mum's worried face. He couldn't.

Nor his dad's. Couldn't remember the first thing about them. Didn't know if they were fat, thin, tall, short…

Panic gripped him. An icy cold shiver of fear swept over him. Why couldn't he remember his parents? Why couldn't he remember his own name?

He tried to get out of bed. If he could just get up, walk about, everything would come back to him.

The doctor gently pushed him back. "Relax, Eric. Just relax."

"That's not my name!" he shouted.

A large figure in black stepped towards them. Eric hadn't spotted the policeman who must have been sitting by the door.

The doctor barred the policeman's way. "It's fine, officer. No problem."

The policeman had a sour look on his face. Not the sort of face that said he was sorry for running anyone down. He glared, took a step back and folded his arms.

Eric glared back, wondering what the guy's problem was. Maybe Eric's head had dented his precious police car. An apology would have been nice.

"So," said the doctor. "You don't think you're Eric. So what is your name?"

Eric opened his mouth to tell them. Nothing came. Instead a great black void opened up in his brain. There was nothing there. No memories — nothing. Panic began to choke him.

His mind was a total blank.

CHAPTER 2

UNWELCOME VISITORS

They did tests. They prodded, poked, scanned, asked questions. They stuck electrodes to his head and he watched his brain patterns on a TV screen. They got him reading words off a card — that had been a bit tricky. They tried to trick him, to find out if he was lying. Why lie? He wasn't that desperate to get out of school — was he?

He couldn't remember school. Didn't know if he liked it or not. Didn't know if he was any good at anything.

He went along with all their tests, trying not to give in to the terror. Tried not to think about the blank space in his brain where his life used to be.

The nurse was kind. She'd told him her name was Pat and he'd remembered. So that was good. And he hadn't forgotten normal stuff, like the fact that he was in a hospital. And he knew what a doctor was, and what a stethoscope was. But he didn't know what year it was, or when his birthday was, or even if he had brothers and sisters.

He hadn't. He'd asked. The doctor said no, he was an only child. Eric took his word for it.

The doctor said he was lucky. Some brain injuries leave people unable to walk or talk. So part of his brain was OK.

Nurse Pat said she'd rung his parents. They'd be here as soon as they could.

7.00pm and they still weren't here.

The policeman went off duty, but not before casting Eric an 'I'm watching you' glare. Another policeman took his place. Eric hoped this one would say sorry for running him down. Funny how no one seemed to care.

The evening wore on and Eric sat, eyes glued to the door, waiting for his parents to arrive.

Nurse Pat popped back before finishing her shift. "No sign on them yet?"

"Nope, not yet."

"I'm sure they'll be here soon."

He wished they'd get here. He was sure that once he saw them, all his memories would flood back. He just needed a familiar face. That was all.

Finally, the door opened. A woman wearing thick make-up walked in. Behind her was a big guy with a thick red neck and a red blotchy face. Eric didn't like the look of him at all.

Nurse Pat looked pleased. "Ah! Here they are!"

Eric stared at the two strangers, waiting for something to click into place. But there was nothing. He didn't know them. Didn't even want to know them.

The woman lunged at him. He thought she was going to hug him. But she shook him angrily. "What the hell have you been up to?"

Shocked, Eric sank back into his pillows.

Nurse Pat pulled the woman off him. "Please, Mrs Penny… he's only just starting to recover."

"I'm Mrs Jackson now!" she snapped, her thin red mouth twisting. "Eric, how could you do that? How could you?"

The big man's face turned redder, as if he wanted to lash out. "You'll get the back of my hand, you will. You vicious little…"

Eric raised his arms in self-defence, expecting a slap or a punch.

Nurse Pat looked tiny as she stood up to the man. "Mr Jackson, please! Unless you stop this, you'll have to leave."

They both stood, huffing and puffing. Staring at him like he was a bit of muck. Eric stared back, shocked, horrified. There had to be some mistake. Surely parents loved their kids. He saw only hate in their eyes.

The woman, his mother, pulled up a chair. She sat stiffly. "Well, what have you got to say for yourself, Eric?"

"And no lies!" the man growled.

It was too much. He thought his parents would hug him and say it would all be OK. But they hated him. And why were they so angry? It wasn't his fault he'd been hit by a police car and fallen into a coma — was it? Tears began to sting his eyes.

"Well, out with it!" his mother snapped.

He forced the tears back. "I can't remember what happened. I've lost my memory."

The man — his stepfather — threw his hands up in despair. "Well, fancy that! The boy beats up an old man, then conveniently loses his memory." He leaned forward. "At least have the decency to own up and show you're sorry."

Eric stared, open mouthed. "What? I did what?"

Nurse Pat fidgeted. "Mr Pe… I mean Jackson. That's not fair. Nothing has been proven. It's a wild accusation."

"What are you talking about?" Eric cried, dragging his fingers through his hair. "Will someone please tell me!"

The nurse tried. "The thing is, Eric, a man was attacked in his home. You were seen running from his house."

His head swam. Jangled words swished about in the blank void of his mind. "What man? What house? I didn't attack anyone!"

"How do you know, huh?" snapped his stepdad, looking smug. "If you've lost your memory?"

"I'd never do that." He looked at them all. They *had* to believe him. "I wouldn't!"

"Well the police think you did!" his stepdad snarled. "The old man's blood was on your hands and clothes."

"And you were seen running away," added his mother. "They've got witnesses."

"But I'd never hurt anyone," Eric said, shaking his head, despair hitting him like a sledge hammer. Tears rolled down his cheeks. "I wouldn't!"

Later, when they'd gone, he lay thinking. Truth was, he didn't know if he'd hurt anyone or not. He knew nothing about himself — or his past.

Maybe his parents had good reason to be angry. Maybe he was the vicious so-and-so his stepdad said he was. Maybe the police guard was to stop him hurting anyone else.

CHAPTER 3

FACES OF STRANGERS

Over the next few days Eric started to feel a bit better. Not his memory. That was as blank as ever. But he felt stronger, and he didn't hurt so much. He was allowed out of bed. He could use the loo rather than a bed pan. Although that had been better than the tubes!

The first thing he did was to stare at his reflection in the mirror. A skinny, bruised-lipped, brown-eyed stranger stared back. He checked his teeth. He had a couple of fillings. He couldn't remember getting them. His hair was dark. Someone had kitted him out with a comb, toothbrush and stuff. He ran the comb through his hair, hoping his brain would remember how he styled it — if he styled it. Nothing looked right so he gave up.

Today he'd been allowed to take a walk along the corridor.

Everywhere he went, the policeman wasn't far behind — like his shadow.

"Shouldn't you be out catching criminals?" Eric asked, feeling really bugged at being watched like a hawk.

It was the sour-faced policeman. He looked down his long nose at Eric. "I'm watching you, aren't I?"

"Why?"

"Make sure you don't do a runner."

It seemed the dumbest answer. "Why would I do that?"

"To avoid being locked up," the policeman said coldly. "That's the usual reason thugs like you do runners."

Being labelled a thug hurt. Deep down, he didn't feel like a thug or the sort of kid who'd beat anyone up. But maybe the head injury had wiped that part of his personality away. Perhaps he was a violent thug — until the accident.

Eric got himself a drink of water and shuffled back to his room. He clicked the TV on and the policeman took his seat again by the door.

"Was it you?" Eric asked him, after sitting watching a quiz programme that he didn't know any of the answers to.

"What?"

"Driving the police car that hit me."

"No, it wasn't. And don't go looking for the sympathy vote. If you hadn't been running away from a very nasty crime, you wouldn't have run into the road and got knocked down — or rather tossed over the top of the car."

101. A number flashed across the blank space of his mind. Then it was gone.

"Anyway," continued the policeman. "Don't pretend you don't know. You might fool the doctors but you don't fool me. You think you'll get away with it by saying you've lost your memory. But you won't. They'll see through this little charade."

Eric didn't bother arguing, there was no point. He was glad when Nurse Pat came in. Her smile lit up the room.

"You're looking much better, Eric. How are you feeling?"

"OK, apart from the big empty space between my ears!"

She looked kindly at him. "Is that how it feels?"

He shrugged, pretending to be coping. But inside he wasn't. Inside he wanted to scream. He wanted that bit of his brain back that told him who he was. What he was. Monster? Normal teenager? What?

The nurse's hand tightened around his. He clung on, like it was a lifeline to sanity.

***

That afternoon, he had a visitor. A man of about 50, thin, tall, going bald, spectacles. He wore a jacket with leather elbow patches. He didn't look happy to be there.

"Hello?" Eric said, as the man pulled up a chair to the side of his bed.

"Hello, Penny. We heard you'd come out of your coma."

Eric made a big thing of peering around the room looking for the invisible person — the other half of *we*. "Did we?"

"Don't try to be smart, lad. You know what I mean."

Eric had no idea what he meant. And smart was the last thing he was — now. Although he was smart enough to sense that this guy was not a dear old pal. Clearly, he was someone else who didn't like him.

"No one's told you, have they?" Eric said with a forced smile.

"Told me what?"

"That I've lost my memory — total blank-out. Like someone has pressed the delete button on my hard drive."

The man tutted. "You waste too much time on your computer games. If you'd put as much effort into your studies, you'd maybe have made something of your life."

He made it sound like his life was over. "I'm only 15, so I'm told. Plenty of time to upload new data. I take it you're a teacher — my teacher?"

The man narrowed his eyes. "You're putting this on, aren't you, Penny?"

The policeman butted in. "That's what I think too."

"Er… private conversation going on here!" Eric said. "You have to believe me. I'm not putting it on. Mind's a total blank — ask the doctors."

"Don't look so smug about it, Penny," the teacher sneered. "It's a pity the bump on the head didn't knock some sense into you."

Eric folded his arms. "So I'm not a star pupil?"

The teacher shook his head. "You're disruptive and lazy. Your work never gets done. And what you do do is always a mess."

Eric pulled a face and looked at the policeman. "I blame the teachers!"

"It's all a joke to you, isn't it, Penny?" the teacher said. "Well, what you've done now is no laughing matter."

Eric sat forward. "Whatever you've heard, I did *not* hurt anyone. Why would I?"

"Why indeed?"

Eric saw there would be no convincing this guy. The silence between them went on and on. After a long session of silence, he said, "Some grapes would have been nice."

The teacher leaned forward, his mouth pinched. "I did bring grapes — but I gave them to someone who deserved them. Not that he's in any fit state to eat them, thanks to you."

"Huh?"

"I brought grapes for dear old Mr Grant. You didn't actually think I'd made a special journey to see you, did you, Penny?"

Actually, Eric did. But clearly no one liked him. He made an effort to pretend it didn't hurt. "And who is dear old Mr Grant?"

The teacher looked him straight in the eye. "Well, Eric, let me remind you. Mr Grant is our former headmaster. The kindly soul was giving you extra maths tuition in his own time. And how did you thank him for his kindness? Let me tell you — you beat him up and left him for dead!"

The policeman leapt forward. "Sir! I must stop you there! You cannot have this conversation until we have interviewed him.

"Huh!" the teacher grumbled. "You'd best get on and do it then!"

CHAPTER 4

ANGER AND HATRED

Eric's spirits sunk to an all-time low. He was, so it seemed, a very nasty piece of work. It was no wonder that everyone hated him. To add to his joy, his parents came to see him again.

"So has he got his memory back yet?" his mum asked Nurse Pat.

The nurse looked sadly at Eric and shook her head. "No, I'm afraid not."

"Well when is it going to come back?"

"We can't say," said Pat, her eyes filled with sadness. "It may come back tomorrow, or next month — or never. We just don't know."

"Well that's a fine kettle of fish," said his mother. "So the doctors are all a waste of space, then."

His parents could have a go at him, if they must. But it wasn't fair to have a go at the hospital staff. Angrily, he said, "The doctors saved my life!"

His stepdad lunged at him. Saggy eyes bulging. "Don't you raise your voice to your mother, m'lad!"

Eric just looked at him. He didn't know if his stepdad had ever scared him, but he didn't scare him now. He met his gaze. Softly he said, "I'm not *your* lad."

A silence fell over the room. Like something bad was about to happen. His stepdad just glared. Eric didn't back off. He met that stare not caring if this bully wanted to hit him. He guessed it wouldn't be the first time.

But they couldn't hurt him more than he was already hurt. Inside.

He was glad when they'd gone. Besides, he needed some answers, and Nurse Pat was the only one he could ask.

"Nurse."

She smoothed the sheets around him. "Yes, Eric?"

"The man — the one they say I... I beat up..."

She looked kindly at him. "I don't think you did."

He guessed she was just trying to be nice. "But we don't really know, do we?"

"I'm usually a good judge of character," she said with a smile.

He got to the point. "He's here, in this hospital, isn't he?"

She nodded.

"Well, couldn't we just go and see him?" Eric suggested hopefully. "Ask him if I was the one who... who did it?"

"We can't just at the moment, Eric. He's still on life support…"

Her words stunned him. He fell back onto his pillows, arms over his head. Surely he hadn't done that to a poor old man — a defenceless old guy who was helping him. Was he *that* evil?

Nurse Pat put her arm around his shoulder, comforting him as best she could. But Eric's tears wouldn't stop. Tears for the old man. And tears for himself.

He must have cried himself to sleep, but he awoke to someone speaking his name. Someone gently touching his cheek.

He opened his eyes to find the most perfect face looking down at him. Soft brown eyes, long silky black hair. So pretty she could have been an angel.

For a split second he wondered if he'd died and gone to heaven. Then she placed a light kiss on his lips and stroked his hair back from his eyes. He suddenly felt very much alive!

"Your poor face," she said, softly. "All bruised. I've been so worried. I visited you so many times over the last two weeks. But seeing you in a coma was breaking my heart…"

He lay there, letting her caring words soothe him. Amazed to meet someone who didn't hate his guts. Clearly she hadn't heard what he was supposed to have done.

"How are you feeling?"

"Not great… er, this is going to sound pretty dumb. But who are you?"

She laughed. Then frowned. "You're joking, right?"

"Wish I was."

Her brown eyes flicked across his face, her frown deepening. "I'm Vicky, obviously."

The name meant nothing to him. And that was bad. How could he forget a girl as gorgeous as her? "And we're… friends? Like, er… good friends?"

She laughed again, nervously. "Don't, Eric. It's not funny."

"You're right," he said softly, stroking her hand, seeing by her face that he wasn't the only one traumatised around here. "It isn't funny."

The doctor on his rounds came by. Eric was glad. The doctor explained Eric's condition better than he could. Vicky listened, her face pale, holding onto his hand like she'd never let him go. He had to admit it was a nice feeling.

She asked questions. Lots of questions, which the doctor answered. Eric was glad she was there.

When Nurse Pat called in later to check his temperature she smiled at Vicky. "He's looking a bit more lively than the last time you visited!"

"Yes! Thank God."

"You know," said the nurse, "the best thing would be not to fret over his lost memory, but fill up the blank spaces with your memories. Share them with him. Give him some nice things to think about."

"I will," Vicky said, squeezing his hand and smiling into his eyes.

For the first time since coming out of his coma, Eric felt a spark of hope. A little ray of sunshine in the blank empty space of his mind.

He only hoped she wouldn't turn against him when she heard about the poor old man on life support.

CHAPTER 5

A THREAD OF HOPE

Vicky visited Eric every afternoon after school. Then on Saturday afternoon, they asked the doctor if they could go for a walk outside.

"Some fresh air would do him the world of good," the doctor said. So, in his dressing gown and slippers, he had a walk with Vicky around the little patch of grass and flower beds outside the building. Some other patients and visitors had had the same idea.

The policeman came too, tagging along behind like a puppy dog.

"Shall we try and lose him?" Vicky said wickedly.

"That's going to be tricky."

She linked Eric's arm. Chatting away, they wove a path through little groups of people, some in wheelchairs. They strolled around the grassy patch, walking in a circles. Ever decreasing circles, until they ended up following the policeman. He turned and glared. They giggled. He gave up and marched back to the main entrance where he stood, arms folded.

"Genius!" Eric said, loving having Vicky around.

Over the last few days he'd learned a lot about her — and about himself. He'd discovered that they were in the same class, and they'd been dating for six months. She told him about the films they'd seen. She talked about their favourite music, played him some which he liked, even though he couldn't remember hearing it before. She told him which foods he loved, and he believed her — for a while — until she said his favourite meal was snails and frogs' legs! He learned that she was fun. He learned that he liked her — a lot.

They found a low brick wall to sit on. It was odd how tired he felt after just a bit of exercise. Vicky held his hand and filled in more of the blank space in his head.

"Eric, you do struggle a bit at school," she said. "I think you're dyslexic. You don't see words like the rest of us see them. I think that's why your school work isn't great. Or it's why you don't want to do it."

"The teacher that came to see me says I'm lazy and disruptive."

"Mr Lord? Tall, thin? Wears glasses?"

Eric nodded.

"I've told him you could be dyslexic. He just doesn't listen." She inched a bit closer to him. "Anyway, my parents like you. My mum says you're cute!"

"Amazing! Seeing as my own parents don't like me."

Vicky fell silent. Then softly she said, "Your stepdad uses his belt on you. Your mum doesn't even try to stop him."

Eric's eyes fluttered shut. It didn't surprise him.

"Vicky, I need to tell you something. You're going to hate me as well…"

She frowned and looked into his face. "Don't be daft. I could never hate you. I… I l… like you a lot."

"You won't when I tell you this."

She took a deep breath. "Tell me, then."

"They think… the police think I beat up our school's old headmaster, Mr Grant. He's on a life support machine. If he dies, I'd be a murderer."

He waited for the shock and horror to appear on her face. He waited for the anger and hatred to blaze in her eyes. But to his surprise, she held his hand tighter. I've heard all those stories, Eric.

People at school are talking about nothing else."

He hung his head in misery.

"Oh Eric, maybe you don't know yourself. But we all know you. You wouldn't hurt a fly."

"But what if I did? Why else would I have been running away from his house? I'd got his blood all over me. Why didn't I call an ambulance?"

"You must have had your reasons," Vicky said, trust shining from her eyes.

"If he recovers, he'll be able to say if it was me or not," said Eric. "And if it was, then I'll take what's coming to me. And I'll be glad that part of my brain is destroyed. I don't feel like I'm a thug now, Vicky. Even if I was then."

She jumped up and stood before him. "Eric Penny you are not a thug! You're the sweetest boy ever. So don't you ever forget that! Do you think I could fall in love with some nasty violent beast?"

His eyebrows rose. "Fall in love? What, with me?"

Her cheeks turned pink. Then she smiled shyly. "Yes, *you*!"

His heart soared and suddenly the blank dark space between his ears had a rosy tint to it.

"I've got an idea," Vicky said a little later, when they went back inside the hospital. Going past reception she said, "You go on and I'll catch you up."

Curious, he shuffled towards the stairs. There was no sign of his guard-dog policeman. Eric guessed he'd nipped off for a coffee. He hung about, till Vicky joined him. She looked pleased with herself.

"What have you been up to?"

"Just finding out which room Mr Grant is in. I'm going to pop along and see how he is."

"Did they tell you?"

"Yes. I told them I was his granddaughter. A white lie, I know. Anyway, he's on your ward, in a private room at the far end."

Eric waited in his own private room. Nerves jangling. There was still no sign of the policeman and Eric guessed he'd be really panicking because he'd lost sight of him.

There was a big smile on Vicky's face when she came back. "Good news! Mr Grant is off the life support machine and breathing by himself."

That was a relief, but he still had a long way to go. "Did you speak to him?"

"No, there are doctors and nurses all around him."

The door opened and the policeman came in. He looked relieved to see Eric hadn't done a runner.

"I'd better go," Vicky said, kissing Eric's cheek. "But tomorrow, why don't we try and talk to him?"

As she nipped past his police guard, Eric's hopes rose. If Mr Grant was recovering, he'd be able to settle it once and for all. Was he a violent thug, like everyone thought, or not?

He gave the policeman a smile, knowing he wouldn't get one back. "Miss me?"

The policeman just raised his eyebrows. "So who do you plan on talking to tomorrow? I heard you and your girlfriend talking."

"My, you have got big ears, haven't you," Eric said, feeling good. Soon he'd know for sure what he'd done, or hadn't done. "I've heard that Mr Grant is off life support. So we're going to ask him if I was the one who hurt him…"

"Oh no you're not!"

The policeman's words stopped Eric in his tracks. "But it makes sense. Once you lot know it wasn't me, you can go looking for the real villain."

"What! And give him a heart attack," the policeman said, folding his arms, looking like he would physically stop Eric from leaving the room. "No way are you going to speak to him!"

"But I have a right to know…"

"Don't talk about rights. You had no right to attack him…"

"I didn't…"

"And you have no right to go anywhere near him. You wait till it all comes out in court. You'll have your say then."

There was no use arguing. But Eric had no intention of waiting till he got sent to court. He was going to speak to Mr Grant. He needed to know. If it was him, he needed to say sorry.

He sat on his bed and stared at the TV screen, making his plans.

CHAPTER 6

BAD IDEA

2.00am. Eric had lain awake for hours. The noise of the busy hospital slowly settled down for the night. His friendly neighbourhood policeman had dozed off in his chair. Eric crept out of bed. He peered along the deserted corridor. No one in sight.

He made his move. Tiptoeing past the main ward where the night staff were busy with a patient, till he came to the private rooms at the far end.

Taking a deep breath, he peeped into the first room. It was empty. In the next room an old man lay sleeping, his face was bruised and pale.

He didn't look like anyone Eric knew. But then that wasn't surprising.

Eric crept in. There was a chart at the end of the bed. It said John Grant. So this was him. The man who'd been trying to help him study. The man he beat up and left for dead.

Looking down at the frail, pale face, Eric saw the old man's eyes flutter, then open. He looked to be trying to focus, and then he said, "Eric?"

"Hello, Mr Grant."

"Eric, what are you doing here? And you're in your pyjamas."

"Yeah, I'm in hospital too. Got hit by a car."

"No! You poor lad." Even though he was bruised, his voice was strong. "Well, I imagine you heard what happened to me."

Eric nodded, feeling sick inside. "Did... did I do that to you?"

Mr Grant looked astonished. "You? Of course not. Why would you ask that?"

Eric told him. Told him about being seen running from his house. The police car hitting him. Being in a coma. Losing his memory. The blood on his hands.

Mr Grant's grey eyebrows drew together. "Well it's all very hazy. You were due to call round for maths tuition. Your work is getting better, Eric, now we've figured out it's the written questions that confused you. You're dyslexic. I don't know why that's slipped everyone's notice for so long."

"Vicky thought the same," said Eric.

"Ah! Vicky. Nice girl. Anyway, I remember someone coming through my door. I thought it was you…" He eased himself up from his pillows, as he cast his mind back. "Eric, help me sit up, would you."

"Sure." Eric stepped forward and helped him upright.

"Give my pillow a bit of a plump, would you. Now where was I…?"

Eric took the top pillow and holding it in two hands, fluffed it back into shape. "You thought it was me."

Mr Grant continued, "Yes, and I walked into the hall…"

There was a sudden commotion. The sour-faced policeman and two security men dashed into the room. "All right! We've got him!"

Strong arms grabbed Eric. Someone knocked the pillow from his hands. They hauled him away from the startled old man, dragged him from the room. Pushed him up against the wall. Hands behind his back. Handcuffed.

"Trying to finish the old chap off were you?" the policeman snarled. "Good job I was on to you. I knew what you'd got planned."

"We were only talking…"

"And what were you going to do with that pillow, huh? Suffocate him. That's what!"

"I wasn't!" Eric cried, as he was marched along the corridor.

Nurses came running. All hell broke loose.

"What's going on?" the ward sister demanded.

"Caught him in the act," said the policeman. "Trying to bump off the old man he beat up."

"I wasn't… I didn't!"

They weren't listening. No one was listening. He was bundled into an office. Pushed into a chair. Surrounded by stern angry faces.

An alarm bell sounded. A patient needed help.

"It's Mr Grant!" Nurse Pat shouted, poking her head into the room, casting Eric just a quick puzzled glance before dashing to her patient. The ward sister rushed out after her.

"You've given the old man a heart attack!" the policeman snarled. "I said you would!"

Eric slumped back in his chair, eyes shut.

Black despair closed in on him.

Mr Grant was going to die — and no one would ever know the truth.

CHAPTER 7

THE TRUTH

Eric wasn't sure how long he sat there. He could imagine them trying to bring Mr Grant back to life. The heart attack would be fatal, he knew it.

A bleak future of being locked up stretched ahead in Eric's mind. Labelled a murderer. A cold-blooded murderer who finished off his helpless victim as he lay in his hospital bed.

Vicky would hate him.

"Take those handcuffs off the boy!"

Eric opened his eyes. Mr Grant was in the room, in a wheelchair, pushed by Nurse Pat. She was smiling.

The ward sister looked sternly at the policeman. "*You*, officer, have the situation all wrong. Please release Eric. And thank you, security, you aren't needed."

The policeman's face turned a funny shade of pink. He didn't look like he wanted to un-cuff Eric, but the ward sister and Mr Grant were staring at him.

Eric stood up and turned so he could take the handcuffs off.

"Are you all right, Eric?" Mr Grant asked kindly.

Eric could only nod. His eyes were stinging.

"You didn't hurt me, boy," said Mr Grant. "I thought it was you coming into my house, but it wasn't, it was two men in masks. I tried to fight them off. It's all very hazy, but I remember lying on my hall floor. I saw you come in — you were so shocked to see me there. You tried to help me. You must have got blood on your hands then. Then they saw you… knew you were a witness. 'Run!' I shouted at you. 'Run!'"

Over the next few days, Eric had visitors, lots of them. His teacher — who brought him grapes and a card signed by everyone in class. A social worker who talked about him living with foster parents — who wouldn't hit him with a belt. Mr Grant, who popped along with some books, a notepad and paper. Lessons continued as usual. And not a police guard in sight.

Life couldn't get any better.

Vicky sat on his bed and helped him eat the grapes. "Eric, is your memory coming back at all? Or is it still a big empty blank space?"

"Still blank," he said, smiling at her. "But I don't need those memories, Vicky. From now on, I'll be making new memories — happy memories! Won't I?"

"You will!" she said, giving him a quick kiss, and then pinching another grape.

THE END

ABOUT THE AUTHOR

Ann Evans lives in Coventry in the West Midlands. She has written around 25 books including the award winning book, *The Beast*. One of her most recent titles is *Celeste*, a time slip thriller set in her home city. Her Teen Reads and Dark Reads titles are *Nightmare*, *By My Side*, *Red Handed*, *Straw Men*, *Kicked Into Touch* and *Living The Lie*. Ann also writes magazine articles on all kinds of topics.